The Duffy Chronicles

Written and illustrated by Barbara Hammond

www.hammondart.biz

ISBN 978-0-9800675-4-5
0-9800675-4-5

Published by Mirror Publishing
Milwaukee, WI 53214
www.pagesofwonder.com

Printed in the USA

For Amanda, Jack, and Kristen

Love

Thanks to my family and friends that supported this project and believed.

This is for my muse - The greatest dog in all the land!

Chapter One
My Birth Family

I don't remember much about my birth mother. I do remember she was beautiful, and I know she was a poodle named Betsy. My father was a very handsome cocker spaniel. That's why they call me a Cockapoo. It's an odd name and I've been teased about it but I definitely got the best of both breeds, so I don't mind.

I have three brothers and two sisters, too. We were so cute when we were puppies. So many people wanted to adopt us. I was the first to go, actually. I know it made my brothers jealous, especially the first born, because he was so sure he would be chosen first.

I kept telling him it didn't make any difference if he was first born, that wasn't how people decided on the puppy they wanted. Of course, we were all just speculating about this process, because we'd never been through it before. But I had heard my mother speaking about how she'd been adopted and she didn't say anything about first born is first adopted. Besides, I have very good instincts.

My sisters were smaller than my brothers and I, and they were very nervous about being adopted. I overheard my mother telling them that adoption means they're chosen, so they should feel very special about that. When someone chooses you, it is usually because they feel a special bond with you and they really want you. So they shouldn't feel nervous, they should feel proud. I didn't want to let on about being worried, too, so I was very glad to hear my mother's explanation of adoption.

This very nice young woman came to see my family, and the minute she walked in she came straight for me. I knew she wanted to take me home with her and it made me sad. Not that she wasn't nice to me, but I knew I would miss my birth family. I was worried about how they would get along without me. One thing I learned about myself very early is that I'm a worrier!

My parents assured me they would all be fine, and I had important things to learn and accomplish in my life. They told me I was leaving on an adventure and before long I would know my purpose in life.

"It is our duty to search out the reason we are here," my father told me, "and more importantly, to enjoy the journey."

My father, Max, was very worldly. He had told me about his life before he met my mother, and it was not an easy one. He started his life unwanted, and then he was given away to a very irresponsible young man who eventually abandoned him. Luckily for my father, there was a very nice lady in the building where he was left, and she took care of him until she could make arrangements with a friend of hers that needed a special companion. She knew Max would be perfect for the job.

So, through that hardship he found his purpose. He met Gordon, an elderly gentleman that really needed a good friend.

My father told me, "When they say dogs are mans best friend, it's true."

He knew instantly that he and Gordon were meant to be together. I asked him how he knew and he told me he couldn't explain it, but you just get a feeling inside that tells you when you have reached the right destination.

My father stayed with Gordon for three years. They lived in a small bungalow with a very small yard and a front porch. One of their favorite times of day was dusk. They would sit together on the porch after dinner just watching the evening come, smelling the air and listening to the crickets. They usually sat there in silence, but sometimes Gordon would talk to Max about how he was feeling or about something he remembered from years before. Max always enjoyed his stories. They did everything and nothing together.

As Gordon became ill, he relied more and more on Max, and he was never disappointed. Max would often have to check on Gordon in the night, just to reassure himself that he was OK. And he was always there to wake him in the morning.

I remember my father telling me about how gruff Gordon seemed in the beginning; grumbling about not needing a dog and how they were too much trouble. But Max saw right through his bluster. He knew this was where he belonged.

Unfortunately Gordon had to move to a place that didn't allow dogs. It was heart breaking for both of them. Gordon didn't want to leave Max, and Max certainly didn't want to see his best friend go, but sometimes you have no control over things that affect your heart. Max put up a strong front so Gordon wouldn't feel too bad about leaving him, and he knew Gordon sensed that Max would be all right. As soon as Gordon left, Max ran away. He told me he felt it was better to search for a new home alone, than to perhaps end up with someone that didn't really want him.

His time on the streets only lasted a short while before he met my mother. He said it was love at first sight! He happened upon a beautiful pond, with bright flowers and wonderful scents all around, and couldn't resist taking a swim. Cocker Spaniels love to swim! But while he was splashing around in the water, rinsing off the dust of the road, someone was watching him very intently.

My mother, Betsy, stood there at the edge of the pond watching this handsome brown dog clearly trespassing on her property, and wasn't quite sure what to make of him. He had a very kind face, with a spark of rascal in his eyes, which she liked very much. Then he looked up and caught her staring at him. They both told me it seemed like forever that they just stared at each other.

Finally my mother broke the silence. "Just who do you think you are to just come into someone's yard uninvited?"

Max got out of the water and shook off before walking over to introduce himself. He was trying to think of a way to explain his situation, and let her know he was not intending to be rude.

"My name is Max." He inched closer as she stood her ground. "I apologize for taking a swim in your pond without permission, but I've been walking for quite a while and it just looked so inviting I couldn't resist."

She didn't make a move, so he started to walk away saying, "I'll be leaving now; I hope I didn't upset you."

And as he turned to go she said, "Are you hungry?"

Boy was he ever hungry! But he didn't want to look too desperate, so he turned to her and replied, "I would love to share a meal with you, if it's not too much trouble."

"Come with me," she said, and started to walk towards the house up the path.

Before the evening was over, Max had met Betsy's family and gotten an invitation to stay with them for a while. A while turned into a permanent arrangement. My father told me he felt completely at peace there. He still missed Gordon and thought about him often, but his job had been completed there. Now he was entering a new phase of his life, and he felt very blessed.

I felt very excited and brave after our talk. I really hoped I would get that special feeling inside from my adopted mother. So with very high hopes I ran to my brothers and sisters to say good-bye. I didn't want them to worry about me, and I was concerned that worrying might run in the family. I wrestled

9

with my brothers for a minute or two, and I nuzzled my sisters and kissed their heads. Then I had to get going because I didn't want to lose my nerve.

The journey began.

Chapter Two
My New Mom

My adopted mom just couldn't wait to introduce me to all her friends. She would go on and on about how adorable Duffy was, and at first I had no idea that she was talking about me. Then I learned that my name was Duffy. No one in my family had a name except my mother and father. We called them Mother and Father, but everyone else called them Betsy and Max. I kind of liked the name Duffy; it suits a boy dog I think. And I had to agree with her, I was adorable! But we didn't really know each other yet, and we had some difficulty adjusting to each other's habits.

My adopted mom, Linda, had never had a puppy before, so she wasn't very good at the house training business. You would think someone would read about things that important before they decided to get a puppy, but it's amazing how many people don't. So just because she didn't know how to train a puppy, I would get punished.

If you don't take a pup out when they have to go, what do you expect a guy to do? I tried to wait until she got home, honest I did, but she was gone a very long time each day. Puppies need to go a lot! And when we get bored we search for things to play with. If you don't have lots of things for a puppy to play with, they will usually find things you don't want them to play with which always causes trouble. She always left lots of water and food for me, but no toys. I don't think she gave much thought to what happens when I drink all that water and eat the food, either.

We shared a very small apartment, which was my first adjustment. I was used to a large house with a lot of grass to play on. We had a pond and lots of flowers, not to mention four children to play with.

It was the youngest child, David, whom my mother was closest to. He was the youngest and in a wheelchair and she always stayed close by his side. I'm not sure why David was in a wheelchair, but he had been born with a disease that made it impossible for him to walk. My father told me that David was that special friend for my mother. She came to that family to be David's best friend.

I was willing to make adjustments, because I really wanted to be Linda's best friend.

My water and food were in very big bowls that said 'woof' on the side of them. I'm sure she thought they were cute when she bought them for me. I think she was either preparing to buy a Golden Retriever, or else she thought Cockapoos grew very large. We don't, you know. We're actually the perfect size for most people… not too small, yet big enough to get the respect a dog deserves.

I'm sorry to ramble on; now let me get back to my description of our apartment….

She always left my food and water in the kitchen right between the counter and the door to the living room. The kitchen had a very shiny tile floor, and it was cool to lie on it when the apartment got warm and stuffy. I was born on May 12th, and when Linda adopted me I was 8 weeks old. A small apartment in the summertime can get quite warm. The rest of the house had a very soft white carpet. I liked the softness, but I have to admit white isn't the best color to have while a puppy is learning, let's say… basic training.

In the beginning I was embarrassed, and I would try to find out of the way places to relieve myself. The closet seemed like a good place to me, kind of like my own bathroom. It was quite large and sometimes I would chew on the shoes while I was in there. Puppies need to chew a lot because their baby teeth don't last very long, and they are teething for months.

Well, let's just say Linda didn't exactly agree with my choices. Good grief - the screaming! You would think all those shoes were made of some special rawhides, for crying out loud. They didn't taste expensive. She didn't keep the closet very neat, so I was surprised that she was so picky about any mess I made. I thought if she had really cared about her things, the closet would have been neater. Her closet was so messy I had to move things around to find the floor. Honestly I didn't think she would mind. But she called me an evil little dog and said that I had destroyed her closet and her shoes. I felt name calling was unfair!

When she finally settled down, I begged her to take me for a walk. I love walks! All dogs LOVE walks! I wanted to show her how it was supposed to be done…on the grass! But she didn't even appreciate what I was trying to teach her. Mumbling, cursing, yanking on my leash, she was being very ungrateful.

Then she didn't even clean up after me, so I was really embarrassed! Even though I wasn't on a leash at my parents' home, there was always someone cleaning up after us. It's just the way it should be. I just knew someone was going to step in it, and even if they didn't know I'd done it, they would be angry with me. Oh, the guilt!

Every day she would leave me alone for hours and hours, and every day I would try to amuse myself. It was very obvious early on that we weren't amused by the same things.

I really enjoyed sculpture. The kitchen had very heavy wooden chairs with interesting grooves in them. Not that I disliked the design, but I honestly felt I could improve upon it.

I spent hours on quite a work of art one day, and as a bonus it made my baby teeth feel great. Then she came home and the hysterics started…

"Oh no! You've ruined the chair!"

She didn't even try to see the beauty in the piece! She got so wrapped up in berating my artistic talents that she didn't look down in time to see the puddle I accidentally left on the floor.

Then ,whoops, boom, down she went. I really felt bad, I have to admit! I would never intentionally hurt anyone, after all. But we just weren't on the same wavelength about my house training needs.

The deal breaker for me was when her boyfriend, Les, started spending most of his free time with us. We didn't like each other from the get go! He used to come over quite a lot and he made it clear he didn't like dogs from the very first time we met.

I couldn't understand how she could be that close to someone and not know how he felt about something as important as getting a pet, before she decided to adopt me. I remembered my father telling me about the young man that had abandoned him when he was a pup, and I was concerned it could happen to me if Les had his way.

I had adjusted somewhat to her screaming and hysterics, but Les liked to hit me. And hitting wasn't enough, first he'd tease me. He liked to play stupid games, like the plate game.

I was used to getting some of Linda's scraps after dinner, even if it was derived from guilt, so I would sit by the table while they ate, staring up with my sad brown eyes, anticipating a taste. Having my father's cocker spaniel eyes really helped with Linda. She always gave in eventually. Les was another story. He would always offer me the plate, but then start to pull it away. If I wasn't fast enough, he'd hit me. What a sicko! Like I'm not neurotic enough… I really couldn't deal with his games. I so wanted this to be where I belonged, but the only feeling I had inside was fear and tremendous disappointment. I know that wasn't the feeling my father was talking about.

Chapter Three
Freedom!

I started planning my escape. I had decided those two deserved each other, and I didn't need parents that were less trained than I was.

Then the day came when I could run to freedom! I was so excited from the anticipation that I must have left 10 puddles on my way out! It made me laugh thinking of those two slipping around trying to find me.

My plan seemed so easy. With no air conditioner in the apartment, she would leave the window open. So I had been working on making a hole in the screen above the sofa, and expanding it each day. Finally my big day arrived! I looked around the apartment and felt very sad that this hadn't been the home I hoped for. Linda was a nice lady, but she wasn't ready to be a mom yet. I hope someday she will be happy, and maybe even find another dog to share her life with. It was time to go.

I pushed the screen and jumped right out of the window! Fortunately we were on the first floor and it wasn't a very long jump because I hadn't even thought about the height. I'm very agile, like a cat, so I easily landed on my feet and ran like the wind!

Freedom! Freedom! Freedom! The sun was shining and I just knew this was the right thing to do. Everything smelled so great. I was soaking up the smell of grass and rolling in it! I stayed off the sidewalks and ran through yards and parks, reveling in the beauty of the day. I chased some squirrels, because I could, and I laughed as they ran up a tree. They're so

stupid, it's hardly a challenge. Birds think they're so smart because they can fly away, but I chased them anyway. Boy was I having fun! It seemed like I'd gone miles and miles in no time at all.

Then I started to get hungry and thirsty, so I slowed down to look for some place to get a drink of water and maybe something to eat. I had avoided people all day, because after all, I was escaping and didn't want anyone to find me.

Just then, out of nowhere, this really nice man knelt down to say hi to me. He had the nicest plump round face and a very calm voice. I liked him right away, but I was still a little skeptical. I had to keep my guard up. But when he offered me a biscuit, which he pulled out of his big pocket, I knew this was a person that really liked dogs. I thought that maybe I could trust him.

I must have eaten the biscuits so fast he figured I was really starved. He said, "Well, little buddy, I know a place where you can get a meal and maybe we can find your family."

I liked the way he called me 'little buddy.' Then he put me in his truck, which was very large and roomy, and let me sit right up front next to him while he drove. I love sitting up front when I'm riding! Feeling the wind blow my ears back and all the new smells; it's so much fun! That was only my second time riding and first time in a truck, but I knew it would always be something I would enjoy.

He talked to me and patted my head. He even scratched my ears and remarked about how long and beautiful they were. I get them from my dad so I'm very proud.

I was sure that what I was feeling inside was the feeling my father spoke of. My new friend kept mentioning this great place where I would get a good meal, and they would help me find my mom. I didn't have the heart to let on to him that she wouldn't miss me, probably not even look for me. I just wanted to stay with him.

We stopped so many times on the way that it seemed to take all day to get to this place he was talking about. He kept getting in and out of the truck, but I stayed right there and waited for him each time. I wanted to show him I was very well behaved. I heard other dogs barking at my new friend and I thought that was pretty rude. Maybe they wished they were in my place. I so enjoyed the ride. I felt we were really bonding.

As he pulled into a long driveway, I heard lots of barking. At first I thought maybe it was my real family. It would be cool to see my brothers and sisters, to see if they were as cute as I was, you know.

But then to my shock and horror, my new best friend was taking me to a place that had all the dogs in cages! Doggie Jail! I couldn't believe it. The ultimate betrayal. How could he do this to me? We were close! I heard him give the warden some story about how he would love to keep me but wasn't allowed to have pets in his building. Yeah, sure. TRAITOR!

Then I noticed she handed him some envelopes as he left and I realized I had been bonding with a MAILMAN!!! My father warned me about them. He said there was a long standing feud between dogs and mailmen. He wasn't sure why, but that it had been going on for many generations, and it was important to honor that tradition. That uniform is burned into my brain. It makes me crazy every time I see one. Someday it will be HIM, and then he'll be sorry!

Chapter Four
Doggie Jail

What a horrible place that was. So noisy I couldn't imagine anyone ever sleeping there. I was very tired, but so afraid to let my guard down. After all that time and effort to escape, only to end up in doggie jail! So unfair!

The warden seemed to know my name, which I found very odd, until I realized it was on my collar. I sat there, tied to a table, while she called Linda.

Then I saw the pity on the warden's face, and I knew I had been right. Linda didn't want me back. I wanted to say, "Hey, don't feel sorry for me, I'm fine by myself. Just let me go, and I'll be fine, really." And for a split second I thought the warden understood what I was thinking. I thought she might go for it... until I saw my cell.

Since I was only a pup I got the smallest cell they had. I cried, I howled, I barked, I made every noise I could manage. No one seemed to care. This was the saddest day of my life. The people at the jail fed me and gave me water. Some of them even stopped to pet me but they didn't release me. I kept thinking, "How could this happen to me? I'm not a bad puppy, honest. I'm just sensitive. I can't deal with screaming and hitting, is that wrong?"

At the time, I was weighing that against being in jail, and I'm not sure which was worse.

It seemed like days and weeks that I had been in that tiny jail cell. Whenever anyone came by I would yelp and jump...

"Hey, pick me! Take me out of here! I'll be good, I promise!"

Sometimes people would stop and pat my head, or talk to me for a minute, but no one took me from my cell.

Then I saw this lady come in with a very worried look on her face. I recognize worry, being a natural worrier. She looked like she needed my help. So I went out of my way to get her attention. She stopped. We looked at each other for quite a while. I liked her eyes, they were a soft brown like mine, and you could sense what she was thinking by looking in her eyes. I sensed, from our connection, that she liked me very much. She spoke to me very sweetly and commented on my handsome good looks. I was feeling pretty confident about this one. Then she just walked away. I couldn't believe it! I really felt we had something between us, a connection.

A little while later the warden came and got me. I figured we were going for a little duty walk. Boy was I surprised when we went into this big room and there she was, the lady I had been talking to earlier. I got so excited that I didn't even notice the big black dog she had with her.

I jumped in her lap, I licked her face, and she just laughed and hugged me! Then I noticed the big black dog! He was watching me like a hawk, and letting me know it.

The nice lady said, "Benson, what do you think of Duffy?"

So I see Benson eyeing me up and down, then he just gives me this 'superior' glance and turns away. What is that about? What's on his mind? I hope I get the chance to find out because he looks like he could be a nice guy. Maybe we could be friends.

After that, everything happened so fast my head was spinning. The warden took me back inside and I was so afraid the lady thought Benson didn't like me, so she wasn't going to take me. I thought he liked me OK, he just had an attitude problem.

"I can win him over, just give me a chance," I thought. And then, there she was again, but without Benson.

I thought, "Did she choose me over the big dopey dog with the attitude? Smart lady!"

The warden handed me to the nice lady, and we walked out into the sunshine. I'd been sprung! Whoopee!

As we walked toward her car, I was so excited I don't remember my feet touching the ground! This was such a happy day! I must admit I was a little surprised that this nice lady would leave Benson in Doggie Jail, though. He seemed like a nice enough guy, and frankly I wouldn't wish that place on anyone. But I couldn't stop thinking about how lucky I was to be sprung from there!

We got in the car and I sat in the front seat. I love sitting in the front seat. That's my favorite place to sit. The seat was very comfy and roomy. If I stood up I could see out the window and feel the wind in my ears.

Then I peeked into the back seat and, Uh Oh! Benson! He had been so quiet I couldn't believe it. This was his car, and he didn't look too happy about me being in the front seat.

I'd been an only child for quite a while and on my own for days. What was she thinking? I'm a Cockapoo and I have no idea what Benson is, except much larger than I am! We're both boys, too. How could she think this was a good idea?

Then I remembered her worried look when I first saw her. Maybe she and Benson need my help. I remembered what my father told me about life being a journey, and finding my purpose. I had to admit it had been quite a journey so far! And I was only three months old!

So we drove off. My new mom and me in the front seat of the car and Benson in the back seat. He didn't seem upset about me, but something was definitely bothering him. Then I realized he was carsick. So he doesn't travel well, hmm. After checking him out discreetly, I thought my first impression had been right, he seemed like a very nice dog. So what was she worried about?

We made a stop after a while and this man got in the car. He didn't seem very happy to see me at first. He spoke to Benson and the lady, and then he just stared at me. He had a mustache and bright blue eyes that were looking right through me, but he seemed pretty approachable, so I climbed in his lap. It didn't take very long before he warmed right up to me. He made some wise crack about the hair on my face growing funny, which made her laugh.

I thought, "I'm not going to be the butt of your jokes buddy!"

But he didn't mean any harm, he was just kidding. Turned out, he was my new dad, Dan. My new mom's name was Emily.

Chapter Five
A Real Home

When we got to my new home, I couldn't believe the place. This was no tiny apartment, it was a huge house. After Benson and I got to know each other a little bit, he explained that this was HIS house, and I was welcome as long as I remembered that. Then he showed me around. The living room was very long with a fireplace at one end, and three big windows that had very deep windowsills. There was a big fluffy sofa in front of the windows, with lots of pillows. I knew I would love napping on that sofa and in those windowsills! Then we went into the dining room and there were two doors that looked out onto a deck with lots of trees around it. He mentioned how annoying the squirrels were and whenever he went out on the deck he loved to see them run away.

Something we had in common!

The next room we walked into was the kitchen. It was huge with an island in the middle, and it connected to the family room, which had really big windows that came down to my level. I could see out of the window into a large beautiful yard with flowers, and it reminded me of where I was born. Then we went down a hallway past a bathroom into an office. Benson explained that this was where Mom worked when she didn't go to her other office. She had a soft futon in the corner and Ben said it was nice to just relax in there while she worked. I was glad to see there was room on the futon for both of us.

We had to stop and rest for a while before we went

upstairs. This was a great opportunity to just talk and get to know each other better. This was so enjoyable! I had a great mom and a great dad, a big brother that needed a friend, and this beautiful big house to share with my new family.

I knew this was a perfect match when I found out the reason they wanted me in the first place. You see, Benson had just moved away from his human brothers, Jake and Craig. He was so lonely he was losing his mind. He needed a friend! So did I! This was working out!

Benson told me all about moving from their home far away, and how physically difficult the trip had been for him, due to his carsickness. But the hardest part was being so far from the rest of his family.

He told me how Craig had picked him out right after he was born. And Benson was born in a barn! Wow, a real country boy. He told me stories about running free without a leash and chasing the boys on their bikes. And his favorite part was running through the ponds! He really loved playing in the water, and so do I. Turns out we both have poodles in our ancestry, and they're known for loving the water. His first home reminded me of the yard and pond where I was born.

Then one day his whole family moved from the country to a city very far from there. I guess the carsickness was something he was born with, because that trip took days, he said, and he was on medication for the whole time. I'm really glad I don't have that problem, because it totally ruins the fun of riding in the car! Poor Benson, he wanted to enjoy the car, but unfortunately he had this condition.

He went on with the story about when they moved from the country to Pittsburgh.

"I liked the house a lot," he said, "and being with Jake and Craig helped me adjust to city life. But I couldn't go out for a walk without a leash on, and that took some getting used to."

Being a country boy, I can imagine how difficult that would be. I much prefer no leash, but you have to obey the laws and I would never want to go back to jail!

His brothers moved away while they were in Pittsburgh and that made him sad. They didn't go too far, but he didn't get to sleep with them anymore, and see them every day. They would come by fairly often to visit, but it wasn't the same. I learned that Benson had a difficult time dealing with change. So when they moved to Philadelphia without Jake and Craig, he began to panic.

I could empathize with him about feeling panicked. I thought I was losing my mind when I ended up in jail! I have since learned that it is not called doggie jail, but the dog pound. Personally, I think jail is a more appropriate name.

Chapter Six
Benson's Breakdown

Since Benson had been in Philadelphia, he had not been himself. He had always been a very easy going kind of dog, very mild mannered and everyone liked him. Even friends of the family, that had invited them to stay at their house until they moved into their new one, loved Benson and never worried about his behavior. Until he started destroying their house. Even Ben (he said I could call him Ben) couldn't believe what he'd done. He said it was just a blur. He would have panic attacks and start ripping bedspreads, chewing doors, and even hurting himself in the process. He was out of control. Emily and Dan didn't know what to do.

In their quest for a solution they had tried many different things to calm Benson down. Nothing worked, and some things made him worse. He told me that they had gotten a cage to put him in when they weren't home. It sounded like a portable jail to me. I started to worry about my new parents, but Ben explained how bad they felt about it.

"They didn't want to put me in a cage, but they couldn't leave me alone because I would panic and ruin something or hurt myself," he said. "I knew what I was doing was bad, but I couldn't help it."

When the cage didn't work, sometimes Emily would take him to work with her. She worked in an office with very nice people, and Ben enjoyed being with them. It was the ride to work he couldn't handle. His carsickness was even worse during this time of his life.

Finally they put him in doggie day care. Emily found a great lady named Carol that ran a dog grooming and boarding service. She agreed to keep Ben during the day while Emily and Dan were working. It came down to the fact that he just couldn't be left alone. It was a very sad time as he recalled, for all of them.

He liked the day care house. There were other dogs to play with, and he was a very social dog. It reminded him of his home when he was a puppy. He told me about other dog friends he had then, and all the children they played with. I could understand how hard it must have been to leave that place.

I remembered the children that lived with my first family. Kids and dogs are a perfect match.

Once they moved into the house we were in, Benson got a little better. He didn't need to go to day care every day. But his panic had turned to depression. He was just feeling so sad all the time. Being alone wasn't enjoyable for him. He wanted a friend.

That's where I came in. Apparently everyone had been suggesting another dog to keep Benson company.

Even Ben's doctor told them, "People tend to get cats in pairs, but not dogs, when in fact dogs are pack animals by nature." He said Ben would be much happier if they would get him a buddy.

They had looked for quite a while to find just the right friend for him but with no luck. Until they met me!

I thought Benson wasn't crazy about me at our first meeting. He later told me he was feeling so down that day that he just couldn't show any feelings. Emily knew he was okay with me because he didn't seem jealous. I'm really glad about that because I like him and his family. I hadn't even met his brothers yet, but I couldn't wait.

Chapter Seven
Settling In

I had arrived at my new home on a Saturday. It was early afternoon on a nice late summer day. I was really soaking up the family atmosphere, and getting more familiar with Benson. I had to do some exploring on my own, just to get a feel for the new environment.

Even though there was a large yard, we still had to go for walks with leashes on. I understood that, but I was a little overwhelmed with all the new scents of the neighborhood, so I wasn't easy to walk with. Benson was almost embarrassed to walk with me, but he tried to be patient, knowing how young I was. He really was a great big brother.

There were lots of squirrels to chase up trees, and I love doing that! We would stop to talk to neighbors during our walks. Everyone was curious about me, and asking how Ben was doing. There seemed to be a lot of warmth here that I hadn't felt anywhere before. It felt right.

In exploring the house I could almost get lost. I was very small still, and this was a very large house. I loved the windowsills in the living room! They were so deep I could nap there and feel the breezes blowing. How perfect this was.

My first night there was awkward. Emily had set up the laundry room for me to sleep in. It was very nice, very roomy, with a soft blanket and even a pillow.

At first I thought, "How generous! My own room!"

I thought that until everyone else went upstairs and I was left alone in the laundry room. Now, maybe if Benson had

stayed with me I wouldn't have minded so much, but if he could sleep in Mom and Dad's room, why couldn't I?

So I cried and cried. I wanted to be with everyone else, not alone. I must have cried so loudly that no one else could sleep either.

First Mom came down to talk to me. "Now, Duffy you have your very own room, calm down and get some sleep."

She petted me for a while, and tucked me into my bed again. I felt better… until she left. Then I started crying again. I really couldn't help it.

Finally she came down and picked me up, with my blanket and pillow, and took me up to their bedroom. She put me down next to Ben and tucked me in. But before she could get into their bed, I was in it. It was a huge bed! I wanted to sleep with them. I had never felt so close to a human before, and it seemed very natural to want to sleep with them. I was the only one that felt that way, though. Benson, being much larger than me, preferred stretching out on the rug next to the bed. He felt the bed wasn't large enough for him to sleep comfortably. I could see that. But I was the perfect size to fit on the bed with them!

We went back and forth for quite a while. Mom would tuck me in next to Ben and I would beat her back to the bed. Maybe because it was getting very late and everyone was too tired to continue, they finally just let me sleep in the bed. As it turned out, my instincts were correct. I am the perfect size to sleep with them, and I have every night since Christmas Eve.

In the mornings, when dad got up for work, Benson would get into the bed with Mom and me until she got up. I loved my new home more than I ever imagined I could.

The feeling my father, Max, spoke of, filled my heart so much, sometimes I thought it would burst. I finally understood what he meant about 'just knowing when it's right.'

As we settled into our weekly routine, I tried to follow Benson's lead. He was teaching me how to pace myself, and deal with Mom and Dad being gone during the day. They always walked us before they left, but sometimes I had trouble making it until they got home. Then Dad had a solution! He didn't work very far away, so he would come home at lunchtime and take us for a walk. Even Ben enjoyed this, although it wasn't necessary for him. As dogs get older they can handle being alone much longer than puppies can. Here were people that really cared about their dogs, about family, and adjusting when necessary.

Benson and I had lots of time to talk and learn about each other while we were alone together. He liked soft toys. He had a puppet named Snuggle that he loved to play with. I didn't understand how a big dog could play with a stuffed animal. I liked hard toys, chew toys. Benson would tease me and take my hard toys and bury them in the sofa cushions! He loved to hide my toys, and sometimes I would chew up his puppet just to get back at him, but it was all in good fun. Most of the time we got along great.

One day I was enjoying chewing on a rawhide in the kitchen, not bothering anybody, just having a good time with my rawhide. All of a sudden I smelled something sort of familiar. Dogs have a very keen sense of smell, you know. So I got up and followed the scent. When I got to the big window in the family room, I couldn't believe what I saw! The MAILMAN! He was walking up the street toward our house. How dare he come near my new home. I had to protect it.

I was barking so loudly that Ben came running to see what was wrong. I didn't have time to explain right then, I had to keep barking to warn that evil mailman to stay away from my new family. Ben must have sensed something awful was imminent, so he started barking, too. I watched the mailman as long as I could from the back window, then I ran to the side window and he was still coming! I couldn't believe he wasn't heeding my warning. I could tell it wasn't the mailman that put me in jail, but the uniform was the same, so they must know each other.

When I couldn't see him from the side window I ran to the front window, and to my absolute horror, he was coming right toward the door! I had never been so incensed since his friend dumped me in doggie jail! I almost burst through the front window, but fortunately it was closed. I was scratching and barking like a maniac, and he didn't even care.

These mailmen are really a different breed. I can see what my father was talking about. They have total disregard for your territory. Although I have to admit, he didn't try to come in, so he must have known I would have torn him apart.

After he left, and I calmed down, Benson wanted to know why I was so angry with the mailman. I explained about the feud my father told me about and the importance of continuing the tradition.

He sort of laughed, and said, "I have never heard of any feud, and I'm a lot older than you are."

Then I told him about the evil mailman that put me in jail.

"Now that I can understand," he said. "Anyone that would put you in jail for no reason must be mean spirited." He went on, "but one evil mailman doesn't mean they're all bad."

"But what about the feud?" I asked. "Don't you think it all fits with what my father warned me about?"

"I can only go by my own experience, and I've never had any reason to hate a mailman," he said, "but if you feel that strongly about it, you have to follow your instincts."

I gave what Ben said a lot of thought, because he was older and had lived a lot more than I. But my own experience, coupled with my father's warning, told me not to ever trust a mailman. We just decided to agree to disagree on that issue.

So every day I would bark and follow the mailman as he approached our house, and every day he would leave. Ben would sometimes just shake his head and walk away, but he never tried to stop me. We respected each other.

Chapter Eight
Brothers

We had settled into a nice routine. I was adjusting to having a big brother, and I think I was helping Benson relax. This was really special, being part of a true family. I knew this was my intended destination.

In addition to not liking change, Benson didn't like thunder storms. After I had been there for a week or so we had a doozy. I couldn't imagine what was bothering Ben, but he was pacing up and down the hallway from the front door to the kitchen.

When I asked him what was wrong he said, "We're going to have a storm, can't you feel it?"

I sat very still for a minute, trying to feel it, but had to admit I didn't. "How can you feel it before it even gets here?", I asked.

"I just feel 'em coming," he said, "and it always scares me."

"Come on, let's play with the ball," I suggested, "you'll forget all about it."

But there was no reasoning with him. This fear just gripped him. I felt really bad, and I didn't know what to do to help him.

Pretty soon I could hear thunder in the distance. By then Ben was panting while he was pacing, and he was reaching full panic mode. I was getting very worried about him and had to come up with something to calm him down, because we were the only ones home, so it was up to me.

First I tried jumping in front of him, thinking that might distract him. Nope, he was in another world, and it wasn't a good one. Then I stood on my back legs so I could be eye to eye with him, and I blew into his face. It was as if I had slapped him back to reality. He really looked at me, and I knew he would listen to me then, so I said, "Let's go lie down on the couch together until this is over."

And to my surprise he said, "OK."

So we got on the couch and I lay very close to him, sort of shielding his eyes a little so he couldn't see the lightning outside, and he calmed down . I was so relieved, because if that hadn't worked I don't know what I would have done. It's very difficult to see someone you care about so frightened.

After that Ben would always tell me when a storm was coming and I'd be prepared. As soon as I settled him down, we'd wait it out on the couch. He always thanked me, even though it wasn't necessary. I figured that someday he would be able to help me if I got scared, and we'd be even.

I'll never forget the first time I met our brother Craig. It was in the autumn and all the leaves were falling from the trees. Ben and I use to love tramping through the leaves when we went on our walks. Sometimes the piles of leaves were so high they were taller than I was, but Ben could still get through them. We both had long hair, and we'd come home with the smell of the crisp fall air clinging to our coats.

One day, as we were on our morning walk, Ben was very excited because he had heard mom talking about Craig coming to visit. He told me that when Mom left in the car that day, she would come back with Craig.

I said, "How do you know that?"

And he said, "I just have a feeling."

I had learned to believe in Ben's feelings, after the thunderstorms we'd been through.

So when Mom left that day Benson got up on the sofa in the living room with me and we looked out the window and waited. I wasn't sure how long we should wait, but he wouldn't leave the window. I didn't want him to think I wasn't excited, too, so I stayed on the sofa with him for hours. Then I saw the car pull into the driveway and we just looked at each other and started barking and jumping. I had never seen him this excited about anything. I was really hoping he was right, because if Mom walked in alone he was going to be so disappointed.

Then the door opened and this guy with long hair tucked into a bandanna, a scruffy beard, leather jacket and big boots ran in and grabbed Benson. I was a little nervous because of his appearance, but I knew it had to be Craig by the way he and Ben were hugging. He called Benson 'Bubba,' and they wrestled around on the floor for a while. Ben was laughing and jumping on him, so I decided to jump into the game too.

"Hey, who the heck is this runt?" Craig asked.

I was a little insulted. Then Mom said, "Craig, meet your new little brother, Duffy."

"So this is the little pound puppy you were telling me about," he said.

He didn't seem that happy to see me. I thought I would eventually win him over.

I found out later that Craig didn't always look so scruffy, but he was an actor and came to town to audition for a part in a movie. I had no idea our brother was an actor. Then Ben told me that Jake, our other brother, was a comedian. He told me about how much fun it was when they all lived at home. They would bring their friends over and it was always like a party, with lots of conversation and laughter. There was always someone around that would sneak goodies to Benson from the table. He said it was too quiet when they both left home . He really missed all the playing around and everyone laughing.

Craig and Benson were inseparable during his visit, and I was feeling very jealous. It was obvious Craig didn't like me and I didn't know how to change that. He would take Benson for walks and leave me home alone. When Mom found out she was very unhappy with Craig.

"How can you do that?" Mom said to Craig. "Benson loves Duffy and you shouldn't just ignore and exclude him like that."

"It wasn't my idea to get the little runt," Craig said. "Why couldn't you get a real dog, instead of this little yapper?"

I was devastated. All of this fuss because I'm smaller than Benson? It just didn't seem fair. Benson didn't care what size I was, he understood we were friends. Maybe Craig was jealous of me. Benson tried to apologize to me, but he obviously couldn't do anything about how Craig felt. I had to find a way to get him to like me.

Unfortunately, while I was trying to come up with a way to win him over, I was feeling very anxious. When I get anxious, I chew, or at least I did when I was a puppy. So Craig would take Ben out to play and leave me alone and I started chewing on the coffee table in the living room, without even realizing what I was doing. It was just a relaxing way to relieve my stress and it did feel good on my puppy teeth. Fortunately no one came into the living room for a week past Craig's visit.

Then one day Ben was walking by the coffee table and stopped dead in his tracks.

"What the heck have you done to the coffee table, Duffy?" he asked.

I was so embarrassed I didn't know what to say. I explained that it had begun when Craig was home to visit and I was so jealous and frustrated because he doesn't like me. I know it's wrong but I couldn't help myself once I got started. Benson just sat there and stared at me with a strange look of concern on his face. I couldn't tell if he was concerned about my anxieties or about what Mom would do when she saw it.

"I do understand how being anxious can cause you to do things you know are wrong," Ben said, "but you shouldn't have let Craig get to you like that. He'll learn to like you; you just need to give him time."

"But it just came over me, honest," I said. "If I could fix it, I would, but it's too late now."

"Well I guess we can just try to keep Mom and Dad out of the living room," Ben said, "but I don't know for how long."

I was so worried about how they would react to what I'd done that I couldn't sleep or eat. What if they took me back to doggie jail? What if they just threw me out of the house and sent me on my way? I would prefer the latter, but I loved it here and I didn't want to be sent away.

When Mom came home we were in the family room, so she came straight back there. She was hugging us and being so loving, and I was feeling so guilty I didn't know what to do. Then I did something awful, that I seemed to have no control over... I peed on the floor! How could I do that? I knew better, but I guess my anxiety just overtook me and I couldn't stop.

Needless to say, Mom was shocked and not the least bit happy! She grabbed me up and got my leash and marched me out to the yard. She was very angry, and for a minute I thought she might just lock me out, but she walked with me and talked to me.

"Duffy, what got into you?" she asked. "You know better than to go in the house! You haven't been yourself since Craig was here."

That was the truth. I must have had the saddest expression ever on my face, because she picked me up and hugged me saying, "I know you didn't mean it and it won't happen again."

That's when it occurred to me that if I stayed on my absolute best behavior, maybe when she did discover the coffee table she wouldn't want to send me away. So I vowed to myself that I would be the best puppy ever! I had to stay here, it was my home and this was the family I was meant to be with. If only I had never chewed on the table!

Unbelievably, another week went by before the inevitable happened. I was getting a drink of water in the kitchen when I heard the yell.

"Duffy!!"

I looked at Ben and he had nothing to say. We both knew it was coming, and part of me was glad it was finally out in the open. So I hung my head in shame and walked into the living room. She was almost in shock, staring at the damage I had done.

"How could you do this?" she asked. "I can't believe it! You are such a bad puppy!"

I looked around to see if Benson was in the room, but he wasn't. I'm sure he didn't want to be anywhere near this scene! Just then I started to run away, and Mom grabbed me. I was shaking really badly, and it must have frightened her because she seemed to settle down a little bit. She took me over to look at the damage on the table and I couldn't stand to look.

"Look what you've done!" she said, but I just couldn't look.

So she took my face in her hand and forced me to look at the table. It was really a mess, with my teeth marks all over the bottom of it. I think Mom was afraid she might hit me, because she marched me into the laundry room, put me down and closed the door.

I sat there very still, afraid to make a sound. Then I heard Dad come home. Oh no, I thought, what will he do?

Mom met him at the door and took him straight to the

scene of the crime. I could hear her screaming about "that bad puppy," but I didn't hear him say anything.

Finally, when she calmed down a little they came into the kitchen where I could hear them talking.

"He is just a puppy and that's what puppies do," Dad said.

Wow, I thought, how understanding!

"But we just had that table refinished and now it's ruined!" she said.

"He's been here for a month and that's the first destructive thing he's done," he said, "so I think we're pretty lucky."

"I can't believe you're being so calm about this!" she said.

"It's done now, what can you do about it?"

Then it got very quiet. The quiet worried me more than the screaming! What was coming next?

Just then Dad opened the laundry room door. I was hiding in the corner shaking. He walked over and picked me up and took me into the kitchen where he sat down with me on his lap.

He said, "I think we've given him too much freedom to roam, while we're not home. Puppies should be somewhat confined until they get past this stage."

I thought, OH NO… they're going to leave me alone in the laundry room every day!

"So, what do you suggest?" Mom asked.

"I think we should block off the hallway and the dining room so they have only the kitchen and family room when they're alone," he said. "And if we leave lots of chew toys around for him to exercise his new teeth, he won't resort to chewing the furniture."

"But what about Benson?" she asked.

"What about Ben?" he asked. "He won't mind as long as they're together."

I was sure hoping he wouldn't mind. I looked at Ben and he didn't look unhappy about this new arrangement. We still had the couch in the family room to sit on if a storm came, and I could still watch for the mailman from there. It turned out to be a pretty good arrangement. But I was still trying to figure out how to get Craig to like me, and I knew he was coming home again soon.

Chapter Nine
My First Thanksgiving

I didn't get to meet Jake until Thanksgiving. I had never celebrated Thanksgiving before, and from Benson's description I was really looking forward to it! He told me about all the wonderful smells coming from the kitchen, and having the whole family there. The long walks through the leaves and watching football. I was getting very excited.

It seemed like everyone was busy for days. Mom was bringing a lot of grocery bags into the house and everyone was cleaning and cooking. I loved all the activity.

The first one to arrive was Benson's grandpa. I didn't even know we had a grandpa! He didn't seem to mind being my grandpa, too. He was more of a cat person, Ben told me, but a nice man.

Then Jake came later that night, and he brought a friend of theirs, Fabrizio. He was the tallest person I had ever seen.

Jake was taller than Craig with short dark hair, and he had the same soft brown eyes as Mom. He seemed to like me right away, and I liked him, too. He called Benson 'Bubba,' just like Craig did. I guess it was a family nickname.

Fabrizio was an actor, like Craig, and they were in college together. Even though Fabrizio was so tall, and he seemed like a giant to me, he was just naturally nice and kind. I can spot a dog lover a mile away, and he was definitely a dog lover.

Everyone gathered in the kitchen, talking, laughing, and cooking. Ben taught me how to just hang out close to the counter and sooner or later when a scrap would fall... bam! I was

getting faster all the time. This was really fun! When Benson told me that it got even better the next day, I could hardly imagine that.

Later that night Craig arrived. When he came in I was sitting on Jake's lap and he was scratching my ears, which I always love!

Craig said, "So you like the little runt, huh?"

I knew that this was going to be hard for me, he obviously still didn't like me.

Jake said, "I think he's a great little guy! What's your problem?"

"I just don't like little yippy dogs."

"He's not that small, and he's still growing so give him a break," Jake replied.

Then Craig totally ignored me and started wrestling with Benson.

Jake was talking to me and scratching my ears. He said, "Good thing people didn't feel that way about him when he came into the family, because he was really a runt! And he yipped a lot, too!"

Everyone laughed, except Craig. I looked around the room and realized everyone liked me except Craig, and that should have made me happy, but I really wanted him to like me.

Late that night, when all the preparations were over and everyone was getting ready for bed, I walked around the house with Ben to make sure everyone was settled in comfortably. Grandpa was in Mom's office on the futon, so we stopped there first. He didn't like anyone in his bed, so we just peeked in and said good night. Then we went into the family room where Fabrizio was settling into the sofa bed. We got into bed with him for a short time and he scratched our ears and talked to us a little while. I really liked him, and it was obvious to me that

Ben thought of him as another brother.

Then we headed upstairs to the guest bedroom to say good night to Jake and Craig. We played on the bed for a while with Jake and he wrestled with us. Then Craig called Benson over to his bed and he ran and jumped into it. I should have known better, but I followed Ben and tried to jump into the bed, but Craig put his arm down and stopped me.

"No runts allowed," he said.

I was really hurt!

"How can you be so cruel to a puppy?" Jake asked him.

I just turned and slowly moped out the door. Jake got up and came to pick me up, but I ran into Mom and Dad's room. I curled up at the foot of the bed, after kissing them good night, and tried to go to sleep. I was exhausted from such a busy day, and so much activity. I had hardly napped all day, because I didn't want to miss anything. But, I had trouble sleeping because I couldn't understand why Craig disliked me so much. Why was he the only one that couldn't accept me into the family? I had to keep trying to win him over!

The next morning, Dad got up very early and took us out for a walk. When we got back I wanted to go back to bed, like I usually did, but Mom was already in the kitchen cooking. I couldn't believe all the preparation and time that went into Thanksgiving! So I just settled into the sofa bed with Fabrizio, because I could see the kitchen from there, and Ben went upstairs to wake up Jake and Craig. Grandpa had been up for hours, and already gone for a walk before we even got up.

Mom made breakfast for everyone, except for Dad because he had to go to work for a while. Too bad he missed it, because the scraps I got were delicious. She made French toast and sausages, and by the time breakfast was ready, everyone was in the kitchen waiting for it. I've never tasted coffee, but it smells really good. I've gotten use to expecting that smell in the morning, whether there's French toast or not.

As soon as everyone finished breakfast, Mom was working on our main event… a turkey dinner. She pulled this great big dead bird out of the refrigerator and I thought, "this is the main event!?"

It was bigger than me, for crying out loud, and really looked disgusting. Benson assured me that when it was cooked I would change my mind completely. I trusted him, but still had some reservations. There was a lot of chopping going on, so there were several opportunities to grab something as it fell to our level.

By later in the afternoon the whole house had so many smells my nose was cramping! It was wonderful. Ben and I would try to nap on the couch while the guys watched football, but there was too much going on in the kitchen to really relax for long. I went in to watch Mom set the table, which she did so very carefully, placing candles on the table and fresh flowers everywhere, like we needed more smells! But it looked beautiful when she was finished.

As it started to get dark everyone was taking food into the dining room, while Dad carved the turkey. Ben was right, it looked very tasty when it was done. I couldn't believe that they even needed extra tables to hold all the food. The opportunity for scraps was huge.

When everyone had settled around the table, Dad asked everyone to hold hands as he said Grace, "Thank you God for this wonderful food and especially for bringing this family together to share our love, Amen."

Everyone said, "Amen."

I was so touched by this scene I said my own little prayer, "Thank you God for leading me to my new family. I am a very blessed puppy, Amen." Then I added, "And please help Craig to learn to like me."

Chapter Ten
The Spirit of Christmas

I will never forget that first Thanksgiving. I still remember how stuffed we were as we sat around the fireplace later that night, while everyone played a game and even ate more! Benson and I could hardly move, but we still fit in a taste of pie that Jake gave us. I didn't want the day to end.

The next day, Dad went to work and everyone else slept in. All that celebrating wears you out. Then one by one everyone got up and started preparing to head home. Grandpa was the first one to leave. Then the boys started packing to head back to Pittsburgh. Boy, I hated to see them go! I don't know how Benson stood it. But he told me that every time he saw Jake and Craig he had new memories that helped him get through until their next visit. Whenever he would start to feel down he would think about how much fun they had the last visit, and anticipate their next one. I knew I wouldn't have any trouble remembering this visit!

When everyone had left, Mom started bringing boxes downstairs from the attic. I had no idea what she was doing until Ben explained that after Thanksgiving, it's time to start preparing for Christmas, which is an even bigger celebration! Holy Cow! I had a lot to learn, and it was all so much fun.

Ben and I sat on the living room sofa and watched as Mom changed things on the mantle, draped garlands over the doors and put candles in the windows. I was very grateful that she secured the candle in my favorite window in a way that gave me room to ward off the mailman. Clearly she understood

the importance of my tradition.

By later in the afternoon, the whole house looked very different. I really liked it. We had been listening to Christmas music all day, and Mom was in a very happy mood. When Dad came home we had dinner in the living room by the fireplace and spent some quiet time together. After all the hustle and bustle of the past few days, this was a perfect evening.

I thought we were finished with the decorating, until a few weeks later when dad brought a huge tree into the house!

"Is this normal?" I asked Benson.

"I don't know if it's normal," he said, "but they do it every year. We'll probably have a party tonight and decorate it with lights and ornaments."

I liked the idea of a party, because that always meant interesting food and lots of people around. I'm a real party guy I was learning.

Just as Ben had suspected, there was a party that night. But the really big surprise was that Jake and Craig came! Even Benson was surprised! We could hardly contain our excitement. And as an added surprise, they brought two girls with them. Since they were on Christmas vacation they came to spend it with us, and to introduce their girlfriends to the family.

At first Benson wasn't that thrilled about the girls, because he was a little jealous.

"Now you know how I feel," I said to him. "At least Craig still likes you!"

He was used to being the center attention when the boys were home, and now he had to share them with strangers. I really liked the girls. Craig's girlfriend was Maria. She was beautiful, tall, with short blonde hair and such a sweet and kind face. She loved dogs, I could tell. Jake's girlfriend was Macy. She and Maria had been friends for a very long time, and now they were both dating our brothers. How strange and wonderful.

Macy was a little shorter than Maria and just as beautiful. She had short light brown hair and a gorgeous smile that put everyone at ease. I felt very safe and comfortable with her.

By the end of the evening, Benson had fallen in love with Maria. He made such a fuss over her that I think Craig was starting to get jealous of him! I secretly hoped he was jealous so maybe he would understand how I felt. I, on the other hand, loved them both equally. Mom and Dad seemed to love them both, too, and by the time Christmas was over we all knew our family was growing. Benson and I now had sisters, too.

My first Christmas was so much fun. I had a lot of things to learn about, initially. I wanted to investigate all the packages under the tree, but I got chased out in a big hurry. Ben just laughed when I got caught, because it had happened to him when he was a pup, too. He sometimes enjoyed seeing me learn lessons the hard way, like he had to. I didn't really mind, though.

There were a lot of similarities between Christmas and Thanksgiving, as far as food was concerned. We had a turkey again, on Christmas Eve, and everyone ate until they were stuffed. Benson and I made our rounds of tucking everyone in, before we went to sleep, but there was such electricity in the air.

Benson told me that this was the night Santa Claus came to fill our stockings that we had hung above the fireplace.

"Santa who?" I asked.

"Santa Claus, Father Christmas."

"What are you talking about?" I asked.

"Santa Claus is the Spirit of Christmas," he explained, "and on Christmas Eve he brings special treats for our stockings."

"But how does he get in the house?" I asked.

"I have no idea, but he's never let me down yet," Ben said.

"Wow," I said, "how am I going to sleep now?"

"Everyone sleeps lightly on Christmas Eve because they would really like to meet Santa," Ben told me, "but he doesn't want to be seen, he just wants you to believe in the true Spirit of Christmas, which is giving."

What a special feeling I had that night. I slept next to Ben on the rug because I figured maybe we would hear Santa together. Then the next thing I knew I heard a loud thud in the middle of the night, and I was sure it must have been Santa! I tried to wake Ben, but he was exhausted from all the excitement and sound asleep. So I decided to go quietly downstairs to see if it really was Santa Claus.

When I started going down the stairs I heard moaning. I couldn't imagine what that was about. Did Santa hurt himself coming in the house?! So I ran down faster, only to find Craig lying on the floor at the bottom of the stairs. He was obviously hurt. The thud must have been him falling down the stairs. I walked around him and sniffed to make sure he was OK, and he seemed to be awake, but barely moving. I immediately ran upstairs barking at the top of my lungs to wake everyone up. Craig obviously needed help, and I couldn't help him. I guess he was right, I was a runt. Within seconds almost everyone was up to find out what I was barking about. I ran back downstairs to show them Craig.

"Oh my gosh!" cried Mom. "What happened?!"

Dad was already kneeling over Craig and talking to him. "I think he may have broken his ankle," Dad said.

"Can you get up son?" Dad asked.

"I'm not sure," Craig said, "I'll try."

So dad put his arm around him and helped him stand up. As soon as he tried to stand he let out a yelp.

"I did something to my ankle."

"Can you put any weight on it?" Dad asked. "Can you move it?"

"I don't think it's broken, if that's what you're asking." Craig said. "But I really twisted it!"

Then Mom said, "Good grief, look at the lump on your head!"

That was the first time anyone had noticed a very big bruise and lump on Craig's forehead.

"I must have hit my head on the railing,," he said.

It was nasty looking.

"Did I make so much noise falling that I woke everyone up?" Craig asked.

"No," Dad replied, "Duffy was the only one that heard you and he barked until everyone got up."

"Wow," Jake said, "good thing the 'runt' alerted everyone before you passed out completely, huh?"

Then Craig sat down on the step and said to me, "Did you do that for me, Duffy?"

I just looked at him, as if 'yeah, it was no big deal.'

But then he reached out and scratched me behind my ear, and said, "Thanks, little buddy."

I didn't know what to do so I licked his face, and he didn't even push me away!

Ben said to me, "Merry Christmas, Duffy, you got your wish. Now everyone has accepted you into the family!"

The End

Printed in the United States
101860LV00003B/157-252/A